METEOR MADNESS!

L.A. COURTENAY

ILLUSTRATED BY
JAMES DAVIES

STONE ARCH BOOKS
a capstone imprint

Space Penguins books are published by Stone Arch Books.
A Capstone Imprint
1710 Roe Crest Drive
North Mankato, MN 56003
www.capstoneyoungreaders.com

First published by Stripes Publishing Ltd.
1 The Coda Centre
189 Munster Road
London SW6 6AW

Library of Congress Cataloging-in-Publication Data is
available on the Library of Congress website.

ISBN: 978-1-4342-9782-2 (library binding)
ISBN: 978-1-4342-9786-0 (paperback)
ISBN: 978-1-4965-0202-5 (eBook PDF)

Summary: The Space Penguins are attacked by a fleet of
starships and only manage to escape by the skin of their
beaks. But they soon start to notice strange things going
on, and it seems there may be a shape-shifter aboard!

Printed in China.
092014   008472RRDS15

TABLE OF CONTENTS

MEET THE SPACE PENGUINS...

CAPTAIN:

James T. Krill
Emperor penguin
Height: 3 ft. 7 in.
Looks: yellow ear patches and noble bearing
Likes: swordfish minus the sword
Lab Test Results: showed leadership qualities in fish challenge
Guaranteed to: keep calm in a crisis

FIRST MATE (ONCE UPON A TIME):

Beaky Wader, now known as Dark Wader
Emperor penguin
Height: 4 ft.
Looks: yellow ear patches and evil laugh
Likes: prawn pizza
Lab Test Results: cheated at every challenge
Guaranteed to: cause trouble

PILOT (WITH NO SENSE OF DIRECTION):

Rocky Waddle
Rockhopper penguin
Height: 1 ft. 6 in.
Looks: long yellow eyebrows
Likes: mackerel ice cream
Lab Test Results: fastest slider in toboggan challenge
Guaranteed to: speed through an asteroid belt while reading charts upside down

SECURITY OFFICER AND HEAD CHEF:

Fuzz Allgrin
Little Blue penguin
Height: 1 ft. 1 in.
Looks: small with fuzzy blue feathers
Likes: fish sticks in cream and truffle sauce
Lab Test Results: showed creativity and aggression in ice-carving challenge
Guaranteed to: defend ship, crew, and kitchen with his life

SHIP'S ENGINEER:

Splash Gordon
King penguin
Height: 3 ft. 1 in.
Looks: orange ears and chest markings
Likes: squid
Lab Test Results: solved ice-cube challenge in under four seconds
Guaranteed to: fix anything

LOADING...

I am ICEcube and you are on board the *Tunafish*, the coolest spaceship in the whole universe. It's cool because it's full of penguins, and penguins like to keep the temperature down. I'm the *Tunafish*'s onboard computer and I can't lie, so you know that this is true.

Yes, penguin astronauts fly the *Tunafish*. Since penguins don't normally fly, and have never been to space before, this is unusual. But NASA decided that penguin astronauts could send useful information about space back to Earth. They trained five penguins, gave them spacesuits, and blasted them into orbit. One disappeared and made plans to rule the universe by himself. The rest lost contact with Earth, and now have only my very large brain to keep them company out here among the stars.

In short, my database says: NASA is a bunch of turnip-heads.

It's a shame that the penguins got lost, because we've learned a lot about space that we could share with Earth.

Fuzz Allgrin invented a nice pickle using Massive Bugle-blasting Blagwit boogers.

Captain James T. Krill learned that being brave is great until you upset a Massive Bugle-blasting Blagwit by picking its nose.

Rocky Waddle recently found out that left and right are not the same thing, except when you're on the planet Mirramirra.

And Splash Gordon has learned not to have a birthday party when space pirates are attacking the *Tunafish*.

RECALCULATING . . .

Sorry, Splash hasn't learned this lesson yet. The crew is throwing him a birthday party right now, singing crude songs about seals and eating too much. I have been trying to tell them about the space pirates for four minutes and twenty-three seconds, but no one is listening.

The space pirates will arrive in approximately twelve minutes and forty seconds. So will the birthday cake. In the meantime, I hope the *Tunafish* crew enjoys Fuzz's piranha biscuits. They won't make the space pirates go away, but they make a lovely *snap* when you bite into them.

Yum, yum. Enjoy them while you can.

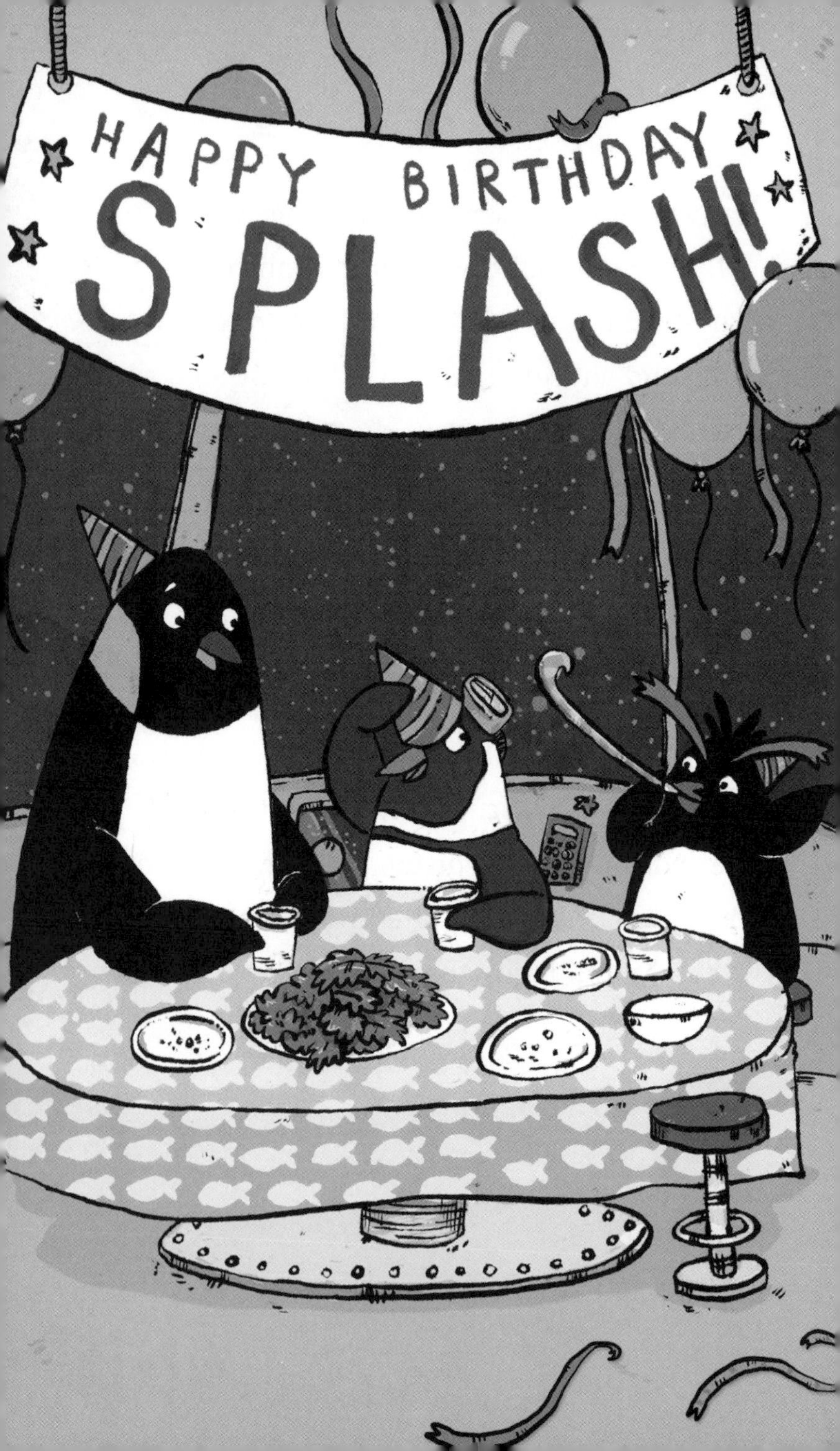
HAPPY BIRTHDAY
SPLASH!

CHAPTER ONE

HAPPY BIRTHDAY, SPLASH!

Balloons and streamers littered the cabin floor of the spaceship *Tunafish*. A large banner reading HAPPY BIRTHDAY SPLASH! hung overhead. Three penguins in party hats sat around a decorated party table, happily resting their flippers on their full bellies. The *Tunafish* cruised along on autopilot.

"Sing that song about seals again, Rocky!" said Splash Gordon, the ship's engineer. His party hat had fallen over his eyes. It made him look like he had two beaks.

The *Tunafish*'s pilot, Rocky Waddle, swept his long yellow eyebrows out of his eyes. He honked his party horn and started singing:

"Oh, seals are fat, seals are mean,
Seals aren't cute like on TV.
We don't like seals — they think we're for eating,
If we saw a seal in space,
we'd give it a beating!"

"Thank you, Rocky," said Captain Krill with a frown on his yellow-striped face. "Can you check the flight instruments? I thought I heard a strange pinging noise coming from the autopilot."

Rocky honked his party horn again and waddled over to the flight deck. "All buttons, dials, and flashing lights on the autopilot are working perfectly, Captain," he reported. "The pinging noise must be coming from somewhere else."

A small fluffy penguin in a large chef's hat came out of the kitchen. "The pinging sound is Splash's birthday cake," Fuzz Allgrin said. He wiped a blob of cake mix off his face.

"My cake is pinging?" asked Splash.

"The oven is pinging," Fuzz said. "The cake is ready."

"Calling all Space Penguins," said ICEcube, for the fifth time in five minutes.

"We're having a party, ICEcube," Rocky said, waving his flippers around. "Stop doing your bossy voice."

"I don't have a bossy voice," said ICEcube.

"I'm sorry, but you definitely do," said Fuzz.

"Let's talk after the cake, ICEcube," said Captain Krill.

"It's important, Captain," said ICEcube.

"So is my cake," said Splash. "What flavor is it, Fuzz? Herring? Kipper?"

Fuzz wagged a flour-covered flipper. "You'll have to wait and see, birthday bird. And you have to eat your space-spinach first."

The Space Penguins looked at the party table. All the piranha biscuits, stellar-salmon sandwiches, and meteor-mackerel ice cream was gone. The only food left was a large plate of something dark blue and squishy-looking.

"I don't like space-spinach," Splash moaned.

Rocky groaned. "Me neither," he said.

"It must be very good for us," said Captain Krill, "because it tastes terrible."

"Space-spinach is full of vitamins!" Fuzz said. "Who knows when we'll next find a planet where we can go fishing for proper penguin food?"

"Vegetables are *bad* for penguins," said Rocky. "We're from the fishy oceans of Antarctica, not a stinky space farm."

"We're not from Antarctica," Splash noted. "We're from the zoo."

"And did they feed us vegetables in the zoo?" Rocky demanded. "No."

Fuzz folded his flippers. "If you don't eat it, I'll put the cake straight into the garbage disposal chute and fire it into space."

"You wouldn't," said Splash.

Fuzz narrowed his eyes. "Watch me."

To set an example for his crew, Captain Krill ate a small piece of space-spinach and drank a big glass of ice water. Rocky and Splash nibbled a couple of leaves.

"Good," said Fuzz. "Now why don't you all play Hide and Beak while I ice the cake?"

Captain Krill covered his eyes with his flippers. "One, two, three, four . . ."

"Calling all Space Penguins," said ICEcube.

"Captain Krill said we'd talk *after* the cake," said Splash, and switched ICEcube off. "The captain's counting. Come on, Rocky!"

During their years in space, the Space Penguins had become very good at Hide and Beak. Splash and Rocky rushed away to hide as Fuzz went back into the kitchen.

"Seven, eight, nine, ten. Here I come, ready or not," said Captain Krill. "Make a noise!"

"You have to look for us first!" Rocky yelled from the freezing-fog room.

Although the *Tunafish* looked small from the outside, it was very spacious with plenty of good hiding places. There were sleeping quarters, a kitchen, an extra-cold storeroom down in the hold, an engine room, a freezing-fog room where the Space Penguins liked to chill out, plenty of big cupboards, a slushy vending machine, a large ice-bath, and a room with a wing-pong table.

After ten minutes of looking, Captain Krill shouted, "I give up!"

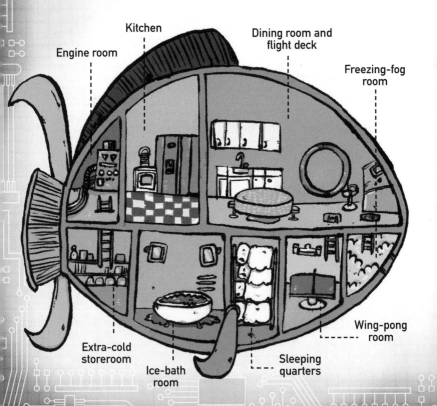

Kitchen

Dining room and flight deck

Engine room

Freezing-fog room

Extra-cold storeroom

Ice-bath room

Sleeping quarters

Wing-pong room

Splash came out from underneath a table. Rocky popped his head out of the freezing-fog room.

"I'm sure I looked in the freezing-fog room," said the captain, frowning.

"Not hard enough, Captain," said Rocky.

As the penguins ended their game, Fuzz waddled out of the kitchen with a huge fish-shaped cake. It was covered in glittery gray icing and topped with candles.

Splash gasped. "A supernova sardine cake!" he said happily. Splash rubbed his flippers together, admiring his cake. "Just what I wanted! Are you sure you didn't borrow the mind-reading hat I invented last week, Fuzz?"

"Who turned ICEcube off?" Captain Krill asked, noticing that the *Tunafish*'s computer was quiet and dark.

There was a stony silence. Splash looked down guiltily.

"No harm done," said Captain Krill, switching ICEcube back on again. "I hope."

"Happy birthday to you," the Space Penguins started singing to Splash, "sushi takeout for two. You look like an orca, but you smell like a —"

"Red alert," said ICEcube. "Space pirates attacking. Battle stations!"

CHAPTER TWO

A NASTY PRESENT

"Bouncing barracudas!" Captain Krill exclaimed. "Space pirates?"

Space pirates were ruthless and cunning outlaws who cruised around looking for spaceships to capture and treasure to steal. They showed no mercy to prisoners. Every spaceship in the universe was terrified of a space-pirate attack.

The Space Penguins rushed to the window. At first, they couldn't see anything. Then, suddenly, they saw a fleet of black spaceships. The fleet's perfect blackness made it look as if someone had cut several spaceship-shaped holes out of the starry universe.

"There are dozens of them!" said Captain Krill.

"Sneaky little kippers," growled Fuzz. "How dare they interrupt my cake!"

"It's *my* cake, Fuzz," said Splash.

"We haven't even cut it yet!" Fuzz

went on. "Don't they realize that this is a birthday party? That's just rude!"

A beam of light blazed at the Space Penguins, dazzling them.

WHOOSH!

Something dark whizzed past the windshield of the *Tunafish*. It sent ripples through the black space.

"Time to get out of here," said Rocky.

WHOOSH!

Rocky jumped into the pilot's chair as another something whizzed at the *Tunafish*. Grabbing the controls, he spun the ship around. More jet-black spacecrafts were waiting behind them.

"Party poopers!" Fuzz shouted.

"We're surrounded!" said Splash.

"What now, Captain?" asked Rocky.

"Straight up?" Captain Krill suggested.

Rocky walloped a button. The *Tunafish* rocketed upward like a crazy elevator. It went so fast that the Space Penguins and the birthday cake were flung to the floor.

"My beautiful supernova sardine cake!" cried Fuzz, struggling to his feet.

"My beautiful supernova sardine cake!" shouted Splash.

"It's a flatfish cake now," said Captain Krill sadly.

WHOOSH!

Another ripple sped through the air. The jet-black attackers were fast. Four of them shot after the *Tunafish*, blocking the penguins' escape. Rocky flipped the little ship like a lucky coin and rocketed back down again. Cake flew everywhere.

The space pirates were closing in, trapping the *Tunafish* like a herring in a great black net. Rocky revved the engines, but they sounded sluggish.

"Come on," Rocky muttered, revving again.

JUDDER-JUDDER-JUDDER went the engines.
The *Tunafish* didn't move. The pirates
crowded in a little closer.

"What's wrong?" asked Captain Krill.
"Why aren't we moving?"

"I don't know!" said Rocky. "It feels like
we're stuck in space glue."

Splash took off his party hat and pulled
down his goggles. "There must be a
problem with the engines," he said. "I'll go
and investigate." Splash quickly waddled to
the engine room.

WHOOSH!

"What is that whooshing noise?" said Captain Krill, glancing around the cabin. "I've heard it four times now."

"Well, nothing's hit us," said Rocky. He revved the engines again. With a sudden roar, they flamed powerfully back to life.

"It's working!" exclaimed Fuzz. "Splash is a genius!"

Rocky pressed hard on the thruster. The *Tunafish* whipped toward the surrounding starships at full speed. Fuzz and Captain Krill flung their flippers around the nearest chairs and hung on with their feet dangling behind them.

"What are you doing, Rocky?" demanded Captain Krill. "We're going to crash right into them!"

"I'm playing a game called Chicken," said Rocky, as the spaceship gained speed. "We're going to see who swerves first."

"That's my favorite game," said Fuzz.

The *Tunafish* raced toward the black starships, hanging still and silent in front of them like a massive black wall.

"They're not budging, Rocky!" shouted Captain Krill.

Rocky accelerated again. "They will."

"Galloping groupers!" shrieked Fuzz. "Show them who's boss, Rocky! We're the Space Penguins, hear us *flap*!"

They could see nothing but the noses of the starships in front of them now. Captain Krill closed his eyes and prepared to be smashed into tiny penguin pieces.

Then the *Tunafish* suddenly tilted onto its side, squeezed through a tiny gap between the enemy ships, and shot to freedom on the other side.

CHAPTER THREE

THE SHIP NEEDS REFUELING

"I think we finally lost them," Rocky said breathlessly.

"That was a brave piece of flying, Rocky," Captain Krill said.

"Thank you, Captain."

"But we swerved first!" Fuzz complained. "That means *we're* the chickens! And the Fuzzmeister is not a chicken — he's a penguin!"

"We didn't swerve," said Rocky. "We just turned sideways and squeezed through a gap."

"We swerved," insisted Fuzz.

"I think they did move away from us, just a little," Captain Krill said in a soothing voice. "And at least they're not following us now. Now how about some cake to celebrate the fact that we're still alive?"

The cake lay in sad, squishy piles around the cabin of the *Tunafish*. Glittery gray icing glooped from the ceiling. As the Space Penguins dug in, their terror of the space pirates began to fade.

Splash reappeared from the engine room. He looked at his cake-eating space-mates with a blank expression.

"Splash!" said Rocky, wiping his mouth guiltily. "We couldn't wait. You don't mind, do you?"

Splash turned to Captain Krill and stared at him.

"Sugar is good for shock," Captain Krill explained. "Thanks to Rocky's expert flying, we just had a very narrow escape from the pirates."

"You mean the pirates had a very narrow escape from *us*," corrected Fuzz. Icing hung off his beak like a sticky gray beard. "There's some cake left under the table, Splash. It's a mess but it still tastes fantastic, if I do say so myself."

Splash went toward a splattered heap of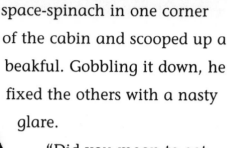
space-spinach in one corner
of the cabin and scooped up a
beakful. Gobbling it down, he
fixed the others with a nasty
glare.

"Did you mean to eat
that?" Fuzz said in shock.

"This ship needs
refueling," said Splash in a
flat voice.

Rocky frowned. "That's not what the
instruments say."

"This ship needs refueling," Splash
repeated.

Rocky hopped out of the pilot's chair.
"Show me the fuel gauges in the engine
room," he said.

Captain Krill watched his ship's engineer
and his pilot head for the engine room with
a strange feeling in his tummy.

"Now I've seen everything," said Fuzz. "Splash eating space-spinach instead of cake?" Shaking his head, he fetched a mop and a brush and started to clean up the mess.

"Do you think Splash is okay?" Captain Krill asked.

"He'll be healthier than a freshwater salmon after all that space-spinach," said Fuzz. "Lend a flipper with that duster, will you, Captain?"

Fuzz and Captain Krill worked together to tidy up the birthday mess, loading the astrodynamic dishwasher, scrubbing the *Tunafish*'s metal floor, polishing the rivets in the ceiling and the walls, and putting the leftover food into the garbage chute. Soon the cabin was gleaming like it had been through a cosmic carwash.

"Good job, Fuzz," Captain Krill said, looking around the cabin. "Tidy ship, tidy mind. Astronauts need tidy minds. It helps us to think more clearly in our dangerous space environment."

"My tidy mind thinks Splash and Rocky are taking a long time in that engine room," Fuzz said, putting the mop away. "Perhaps one of us should check on them."

The doors slid open.

"There you are!" said Captain Krill, as Splash and Rocky entered the cabin together. "Anything to report?"

"This ship needs refueling," said Rocky.

"This ship needs refueling," said Splash.

"It sounds like this ship needs refueling, Captain," said Fuzz.

Captain Krill sighed. "Fine, we'll dock and refuel as soon as we can. ICEcube, is the nearest planet a friendly one?"

"The planet Kroesus," said ICEcube. "Population: four billion. Known primarily for its spacetanium mines, Kroesus produces more than three-quarters of the spacetanium supply in the entire universe. Spacetanium is the strongest, lightest metal in the cosmos and is very valuable. Kroesus was robbed ten thousand times a year until it created a unique security system to protect itself from pirates. Its inhabitants are small, yellow, and unfriendly."

"If I'd been robbed ten thousand times a year, I'd be unfriendly, too," said Captain Krill.

"What kind of unique security system?" asked Fuzz.

"Mechanical meteors orbit the planet at fifteen thousand miles an hour," ICEcube replied. "Every visitor to Kroesus must pass a series of security checks. If the security checks are satisfactory, the meteors are frozen in midair and ships can land safely. If the visitors fail the security checks, the meteors burst into flames, setting fire to their ships."

"This ship needs refueling," said Splash.

"This ship needs refueling," said Rocky.

"We heard you the first time," said Captain Krill. "Set the coordinates for Kroesus, Rocky. And I really hope we're not pelted with mechanical meteors today."

CHAPTER FOUR

SPACE-SPINACH SANDWICH

Rocky settled down at the controls of the *Tunafish*. "Destination: planet Kroesus," he said, setting the coordinates. "Estimated duration of flight: three hours."

"Estimated time of arrival: twenty-five hundred hours, Kroesus time," said Splash. "Check."

Captain Krill watched his ship's engineer and his pilot. He couldn't put his flipper on it, but something strange was going on with them.

"Everything okay, you two?" he asked.

Rocky kept his eyes trained on the flight instruments. Splash looked at Captain Krill without flipping up his goggles.

"Dinner!" Fuzz shouted, bringing out a large plate of freshly defrosted space-spinach and a selection of fish sandwiches. "Sorry it's only sandwiches, but we did just have a massive birthday lunch."

"Destination: planet Kroesus," said Rocky, not moving.

"Estimated duration of flight: two hours and fifty-nine minutes," added Splash.

"Estimated time of arrival: twenty-five hundred hours, Kroesus time," said Rocky.

"Check," said Splash.

Fuzz set the sandwiches down as Captain Krill took his place at the table. Then Fuzz waddled over to Rocky and Splash with his flippers on his hips. "I said, *dinner*!" The Little Blue penguin shouted so loudly that a couple of red flashing lights on the flight deck started flashing a little faster.

"This ship needs refueling," Rocky and Splash said together.

"So do you, you ditzy dolphins," Fuzz said. "Get to that table at once, unless you want a kung-fu chop in the guts from the Fuzzmeister!"

Rocky and Splash turned away from the controls and waddled toward the table. They were moving strangely, as if they'd forgotten how their bodies worked.

"Who wants a sandwich?" said Captain Krill, as Rocky and Splash sat down.

"Space-spinach first," Fuzz interrupted. "Don't complain. It's good for you and —"

Rocky and Splash both shot out their flippers. They scooped up so much space-spinach that there was none left for the captain or Fuzz. Splash tipped it all straight into his mouth. Rocky pulled a sandwich apart, took out the fish that was sitting inside, and replaced it with a lump of space-spinach. Then he put the bread back together again. Blue space-spinach juice oozed out of the sandwich and dribbled down Rocky's front as he munched it up.

"That is the most disgusting thing I've ever seen," said Fuzz. He gazed at the fish lying abandoned on the table. "What's the matter with you two?"

"Is there any more space-spinach, Fuzz?" asked Captain Krill.

"Not you as well, Captain!" Fuzz said in shock. "You're supposed to eat space-spinach, but you're not supposed to *like* it!"

"I don't like it," Captain Krill assured his chef. "But I'm prepared to do my duty and eat it. And there's none left."

Splash wiped the empty plate with his flipper, then put his flipper in his beak.

"I'll fetch some more from the extra-cold storeroom," Fuzz said. Firing a confused look at Rocky and Splash, he waddled out of the cabin.

"Destination: planet Kroesus," said Rocky, heading back to the flight deck. "Estimated duration of flight: two hours and forty-three minutes. Estimated time of arrival: twenty-five hundred hours, Kroesus time."

"Check," said Splash, waddling after him.

Captain Krill chewed his solar-herring sandwich thoughtfully.

Fuzz headed deep into the belly of the *Tunafish*. Thanks to NASA, the extra-cold storeroom held spare supplies of pretty much everything, from spacesuits to salmon pâté.

"Eating space-spinach," Fuzz muttered to himself. "Enjoying space-spinach. *Guzzling* space-spinach. I can't believe I'm getting more of the stuff. I thought it'd take months to go through all of it."

He flipped open the hatch to the storeroom, enjoying the chilly blast as it ruffled through his feathers.

"Space-spinach," he said thoughtfully to himself, looking around. "Where did I put it?"

His eyes swept past jars of pickled space squid, tins of star whale blubber, flipper brushes, oxygen tanks, ice cubes, boxes of wing-pong balls, bottles of feather conditioner, and two pairs of penguin feet, pointing straight up at the ceiling.

"Big beluga bottoms, NASA," Fuzz said out loud, staring at the feet in surprise.

"I know you packed spare supplies of everything, but when are we going to need those?"

Fuzz heard the door slide open. His eyes widened as he took in the shadowy stranger in front of him. Then an extra layer of coldness stole over him and everything went black.

CHAPTER FIVE

OOH, THAT'S COLD

Captain Krill was about to go and try to find where Fuzz had gone when the Little Blue penguin came back into the cabin. He was carrying so much frozen space-spinach that he could hardly see where he was going.

"Destination: planet Kroesus," said Rocky from the flight deck. "Estimated duration of flight: two hours and thirty-one minutes."

"Estimated time of arrival: twenty-five hundred hours, Kroesus time," said Splash.

Captain Krill followed Fuzz into the kitchen.

"Thank goodness you're back, Fuzz," he said. "There is something seriously wrong with Splash and Rocky. It's all 'destination' this, 'estimated time of arrival' that. If I hear how long until we reach Kroesus one more time, I might go crazy."

"This ship needs refueling," said Fuzz, putting the space-spinach away in the kitchen's freezer.

"Believe me, I know that," said Captain Krill. "I think their behavior has something to do with those pirates. Don't you think it's odd that the pirates attacked us, but then disappeared without robbing us or stealing our ship?"

Fuzz took a lump of frozen space-spinach and popped it into his beak. There was a crunching sound as he chewed it up.

"Does it taste better frozen?" asked Captain Krill. "It can't taste much worse. Listen, Fuzz — we have to do something. Why didn't Splash want any birthday cake? Why did Rocky change his mind like that about us needing fuel? And our destination is bothering me for some reason. Why are we going to Kroesus? I'm sure that the answer to all of this is right under my beak. I just have to look harder."

Captain Krill clapped his flippers together. "I know! I'll go down to the engine

room to see for myself just how much fuel we have left. I don't mean to say that I don't trust Rocky and Splash, but . . . "
He stopped and smoothed back his yellow ear patches. "Okay," he said, "I don't trust Rocky and Splash. But I'll trust my own eyes. If we're really out of fuel, then I can chalk up their odd behavior to a simple case of space sickness."

Leaving Fuzz to put away the rest of the space-spinach, Captain Krill waddled back into the cabin.

"Destination: planet Kroesus," said Rocky.

"Estimated duration of flight: two hours and twenty-five minutes," said Splash.

"Let me guess," said Captain Krill irritably. "Estimated time of arrival: twenty-five hundred hours, Kroesus time?"

"Check," said Splash.

Do we really need to be heading for this Kroesus place, with its endless spacetanium mines and its deadly mechanical meteor defense system? Captain Krill wondered, waddling toward the engine room as fast as he could. *What if we don't pass the security checks? We'll be blown out of the sky!*

He opened the doors. The engines rumbled loudly around him as he headed for the fuel gauges. He checked the readouts for each one.

LOW, read one. VERY LOW, read another.

Captain Krill felt guilty. He and his *Tunafish* crew had been through a lot during

their time in space. Why was he doubting the loyalty of his pilot and his ship's engineer like this?

NOT LOW AT ALL, read the third.

PRACTICALLY FULL, read the fourth.

WHY ARE YOU CHECKING THE FUEL GAUGES? read the fifth and final one. WE'RE FINE FOR ANOTHER HALF A MILLION LIGHT-YEARS. YOU DO YOUR JOB AND WE'LL DO OURS.

Captain Krill gasped. He was right! There *was* something fishy going on. And it wasn't Fuzz's solar-herring sandwiches!

A cold breeze blew over the captain's feet. He turned around.

A smoky, dog-like creature stood in front of him on its hind legs. It had a long black snout, short black fur, and eyes that didn't reflect any light. It was so black that the captain wondered if he was looking at a shadow.

The creature shimmered in the air. Captain Krill backed up against the fuel gauges as it floated toward him.

Black smoke crept over his toes. "Ooh, that's cold," he said.

Then he didn't say anything.

CHAPTER SIX

SHAPE-SHIFTERS

Captain Krill opened his eyes and stared at a line of metal rivets over his head. Where was he? He got to his feet and glanced at the bottles, spacesuits, tins, and boxes of wing-pong balls stacked around him. He was in the extra-cold storeroom with Rocky, Splash, and Fuzz.

"What happened?" he asked, rubbing his eyes with his flippers.

"We were hoping you could tell us that," Rocky said.

"Is my birthday cake okay?" asked Splash.

"You didn't want your birthday cake," Fuzz said.

Splash looked shocked. "Of course I wanted my birthday cake! I chose it!"

Rocky shook his head so hard his feathery eyebrows flapped like socks on a windy washing line. "You didn't, Splash. We all saw you eat a pile of space-spinach instead of a piece of cake."

They all started talking at once.

"And then you said the ship needed refueling —"

"There is no *way* I would eat yucky space-spinach instead of cake. I'd rather eat my own flippers —"

"*Enough!*" Captain Krill commanded. "Something weird is going on here, and I think I know what. Remember when those pirates attacked us? And there were those four big whooshes? It must have been the sound of the pirates teleporting aboard the *Tunafish*."

"You mean, they've beamed their way on to our ship?" said Rocky. "But we haven't seen any extra passengers!"

"That's because *these* pirates are shape-shifters," Captain Krill said. He clasped his flippers behind his back and paced back and forth. "Aliens that take on the shape of other creatures. They're famous for loving space-spinach. They got Splash first. Then Rocky. Then Fuzz. Now they've got me as well."

"You mean when Rocky and Splash started acting weird, it wasn't them at all?" said Fuzz. "It was these shape-shifting things?"

"Exactly," Captain Krill said.

"Thank haddock for that," said Fuzz. "Splash and Rocky's conversation was a lot more boring than usual."

"Hey!" Rocky and Splash said together.

Captain Krill tried to turn the handle of the extra-cold storeroom door. It didn't move.

"We're locked in," he said. "So right now, four aliens that look exactly like us are flying the *Tunafish* toward the extremely rich planet Kroesus."

"What do they want to go there for?" asked Rocky.

"To rob it, of course!" said Splash. "Sometimes I think you have a herring for a brain, Rocky."

"They're going to pretend to be four innocent penguin explorers needing fuel," said Captain Krill. "They will get through the security checks and land on Kroesus, then probably shape-shift into Kroesans. They'll turn off the mechanical meteor defense system and bring in that big fleet of black ships to steal everything they can find."

Fuzz gasped. "It'll be the crime of all time," he said, "and we'll be the suspects!"

"It's our duty to protect the universe and our good name, and stop these villains," said Captain Krill. "One for all . . ."

"And all for fish!" cried the others, slapping flippers. The sound echoed around the storeroom.

"But we're locked in!" said Rocky. "We can't stop anybody!"

Captain Krill waddled over to the communication button on the wall of

the extra-cold storeroom and pressed it.
"ICEcube? Can you hear me?"

"Loud and clear, Captain."

"Can you get us out of here?"

"No. The locks on the doors are controlled by NASA-issue keys only, which are kept in the main cabin."

"So much for your mega-brain, ICEcube," Fuzz grumbled. "What can you tell us about these shape-shifting space-invaders aboard our ship?"

"They are called Dogmutts and they are the most fearsome space pirates in the universe," said ICEcube. "They are cunning, dangerous, determined, and unstoppable."

"Nothing stops the Fuzzmeister," said Fuzz, striking a ninja penguin pose.

Captain Krill peered thoughtfully through the storeroom window. "If we can't open the inside door," he said, "we'll have to open the outside one instead."

The Space Penguins examined the door in the wall of the extra-cold storeroom. It led to an airlock, which opened out into the inky blackness of space itself.

"I like your thinking, Captain," said Fuzz.

"I don't!" Rocky protested. "He means we go outside, and that's real space out there!"

"It's our only choice," Captain Krill said. He pointed a flipper at the row of spare spacesuits hanging up by the tins of star whale blubber. "Get yourselves suited up. We're going to spacewalk underneath the *Tunafish* and give those Dogmutts a real birthday surprise!"

CHAPTER SEVEN

SPACEWALK!

The Space Penguins put on the spacesuits
and switched on the microphones inside
their helmets. They shuffled into the airlock
and shut the door that led back into the
extra-cold storeroom. Now only one door
stood between them and the starry void of
space.

"Counting one, two, three," said Captain
Krill.

"Very good, Captain," Rocky said. "Four
and five come next."

"I'm checking the microphones, Rocky,"
said the captain. "Can everyone hear me?"

Rocky, Fuzz, and Splash all gave the
flippers-up.

"We need to tie ourselves together
before we go out there," said the captain.
"Otherwise we'll float away."

Floating off alone into space was a
horrible thought. The Space Penguins
worked quickly, looping a strong piece of
steel rope through their space belts and
double-checking the knots.

"Ready?" said Captain Krill at last.

"As ready as a guppy in a grill pan," Fuzz said. "Time to show those devilish Dogmutts what the Space Penguins are made of!"

"You are holding on to me, right, Splash?" checked Rocky.

"As tight as a tadpole," Splash promised.

"Tadpoles don't have anything to hold on with!" Rocky said.

"Okay, as tight as a trout."

Captain Krill turned the great wheel lock on the external door and the Space Penguins stepped out into nothingness.

Although penguins are perfect for spacewalking, with their natural abilities in weightless, freezing environments, the enormous darkness made the *Tunafish* crew feel very small and helpless. Space had never looked so spacious. The stars were extra bright. The silence was deep.

Holding on tight to the rope, Captain Krill clanged his magnetic boots against the metal shell of the *Tunafish*. He stuck there like a snail.

"I'm pleased to say that the boots work," he said into his helmet microphone. "Try to walk quietly, crew. We don't want the Dogmutts to hear us coming. We'll enter through the external airlock door in the freezing-fog room. That way we can surprise them in the cabin."

The Space Penguins were a strange sight as they climbed under the belly of the *Tunafish*, hanging upside down like a row of bats. Below them, the stars twinkled and glowed.

"This is so weird," Rocky said happily. "I'm upside down, but I feel like I'm the right way up. It's like swimming in a crazy ocean out here."

A large planet lay straight ahead of them, thousands of scary mechanical meteors orbiting it like moons. Kroesus's defense system was hard at work. It looked very unwelcoming, dangerous, and too close for comfort. The Space Penguins were running out of time.

Splash's foot suddenly bumped against something. He tugged on the rope to stop everyone else as he stared at the object beside his feet.

"What have you found, Splash?"
asked the captain.

Splash plucked the thing from the
underside of the ship and held it up. It
was shaped like a tiny jellyfish, with metal
tentacles and a winking lens.

"I've got no idea," he said, puzzled.

"I think I've seen that before," said Rocky.

"Let's worry about it when we get back
inside," said Fuzz. "We're nearly at the door
to the freezing-fog room, guys. We're going

to give those Dogmutts a bashing they'll never forget!"

The door opened smoothly, then clicked shut behind the Space Penguins. They gave themselves a couple of minutes in the airlock to get used to the feeling of gravity again. Then they opened the door into the freezing-fog room. They were safely back on board.

"That was great," said Rocky, as they wriggled out of their spacesuits and untied themselves. "We should do that more often."

Captain Krill put his flipper on the hatch handle. "Ready?" he quietly asked the others. They all nodded. "Go!"

The Space Penguins burst through the hatch and ran into the cabin, flippers raised and ready. Startled, the invaders quickly jumped out of their seats. There was a moment of frozen silence as the Dogmutt penguins and the real penguins gazed at each other.

"This is freaky," said Splash, staring at the Dogmutt Splash.

"I am seriously handsome," said Rocky, staring at the Dogmutt Rocky and preening his eyebrows.

"This ship needs refueling," said the Dogmutt Captain Krill.

"*Fight!*" shouted Fuzz.

With a whirl of feet and flippers, the Space Penguins charged at the impostors.

"I've got one!" yelled Rocky.

"Get off me, you winkle-head!" shouted Splash. "I'm the real Splash!"

"This ship needs refueling," said the Dogmutt Fuzz.

"You mutant mirror! You dirty double!" The real Fuzz leaped onto the Dogmutt Fuzz. "I'd never say anything as boring as that!"

WHAM! BAM! SLAM! As the Space
Penguins rolled and tumbled, wriggled
and wrestled with the Dogmutt invaders, it
became harder to tell who was who. Outside
the window, Kroesus's robot security meteors
flared and danced in the sky.

"This is Kroesus calling," crackled the
communication speaker. "State your
business. I repeat, state your business."

"This ship needs refueling," said the Dogmutt Rocky smoothly, fighting off Captain Krill with one flipper.

"Security check one," said the communication speaker. "Begin weapon scan."

"Wait!" yelled Rocky. "We've been boarded by pirates! Get off me, Splash! Splash? That is you, right?"

"I'm over here!" Splash yelled.

It was getting more and more difficult to see what they were doing. Two Fuzzes, two Rockys, two Splashes, two captains — eight penguins, flippers flying, feet waddling, bellies bumping. It was like fighting full-length mirrors.

"This is madness!" shouted Splash, battling as hard as he could.

"This impostor captain is strong!" Rocky shouted, fighting Captain Krill.

"I'm not an impostor," yelled the captain. He pulled hard on Rocky's eyebrows. "I'm the real deal!"

Rocky fought harder. "How do I know you're telling the truth?"

The Space Penguins — or maybe the Dogmutts — were forced backward.

"Good effort, Splash!" one Splash shouted at the other Splash.

"That's *you*, you feather-brained

flounder!" Fuzz pummeled at everything within reach of his tiny flippers. "How can you congratulate yourself?"

"You do it all the time," Rocky said.

"Not —" *WHAM!* "when —" *POW!* "I'm —" *CHONK!* "fighting —" *KLANG!* "shape-shifters!"

The Dogmutts — or maybe the Space Penguins — were losing the battle. With one final shove they tumbled down into the wing-pong room. The hatch closed with a click and there was the grating sound of a NASA-issue key turning in the lock.

CHAPTER EIGHT

BURD FLOO

The Space Penguins sat glumly in the wing-pong room.

"That went well," said Rocky.

"No, it didn't," Fuzz said. "With all that confusion in the cabin, we're prisoners again. I'm so mad that I could wrestle a rabid rhinoceros."

Rocky rolled his eyes. "I was joking."

"It's no joking matter!" said Fuzz. "And we don't even have any wing-pong balls to play with."

Captain Krill stood with one yellow ear patch pressed to the locked wing-pong room hatch. "The good news is the Kroesans haven't shut down their meteor defense system yet," he reported, as he listened to the Dogmutts in the cabin above. "Rocky alerted Kroesus when he shouted out that we had space pirates on board. They haven't let us in."

"That's good news?" said Rocky. "We're still moving! In half an hour, we'll hit the Kroesan atmosphere and burst into fish-flavored flames!"

"There's bad news, too," said the captain. "The Dogmutts are planning to fly right through the meteors and land on Kroesus anyway."

"That's impossible!" cried Rocky. "Even I couldn't do it!"

"Well, then let us all die as bravely as barnacles," said Fuzz in a noble voice.

"I'd rather *live* as bravely as a penguin," Splash said. "But first I want to figure out how this ended up on our ship." He waved the jellyfish-like thing he'd plucked off the *Tunafish* during their spacewalk. "It's a camera. I've been checking its memory banks. It looks like it's been transmitting information about us ever since we left Beaky Wader's *Death Starfish* space station three months ago."

"I knew I'd seen it before," Rocky said. "I found it on my belt in the *Death Starfish* space port and flicked it off!"

"Ever since Beaky asked us to live with him on his space station and we turned him down, he's been after us," said Captain Krill thoughtfully. "He must have attached the camera to the *Tunafish*. It explains how he knew where we were that time he attacked us and we crash-landed. It also explains how he found us at the Superchase Space

Race. He's been watching us this whole time!"

"It hasn't helped him much," said Fuzz. "We still wrecked his space station and ruined his chances of winning the Superchase Space Race, not to mention wrecking his special armor and blowing him up a couple of times. I'm guessing Beaky Wader really hates us."

"Aren't we supposed to call him 'Dark' Wader now?" asked Splash. "I know he used to be our space-mate aboard the *Tunafish*, but these days he's the most evil villain in the universe."

"I'd sooner give him a collar and leash and call him Bark Wader," said Fuzz.

"Or give him a lovely singing voice," said Rocky. "Then he'd be Lark Wader."

"Or we could cover him in grass," said Splash, "and make him Park Wader."

Rocky, Fuzz, and Splash all roared with

laughter. "Pull yourselves together, crew," Captain Krill ordered. "In thirty minutes we'll all be deep-fried penguin puffs. We need a plan."

After a few more chuckles, Splash stopped laughing and straightened his goggles. He waved the jellyfish-cam in the air. "I have it, Captain," he said. "Let's send Beaky a message he can't resist."

"What sort of message?" asked Captain Krill.

"We'll tell him that the Space Penguins are vulnerable to attack," said Splash. "When he turns up with guns blazing to blow us out of the sky, the Dogmutts will have to turn away from the flaming meteors in order to fight him off."

"There's a flaw in that plan somewhere," said the captain. "But I can't put my flipper on it."

"It'll be easy as pie — just like taking

doughnuts from a dolphin," said Fuzz happily. "If dolphins liked doughnuts."

"Thirty minutes until impact," said ICEcube.

"Flaw or no flaw, it's the only plan we have," Captain Krill said, making the decision. "Send the message, Splash."

Several million light-years away, a shiny silver Squid-G spacecraft was cruising along through the vastness of space. It looked like a tiny silver bug floating on an enormous black ocean. A large armor-plated penguin hungrily scanned the skies through the windshield.

"Where are they, Crabba?" demanded Dark Wader. "Find those Space Penguins for me. I will skewer them on a stick and barbecue them. I will use their beaks as cutlery handles. I will pull out their feathers one by one and make them dance the tango on a bed of hot coals! Revenge will be *mine*!"

"You've been saying that for weeks, boss," said the small scaly alien sitting on Dark Wader's shoulder. "Let's admit that we've lost them and go home."

"*Never!*" roared Dark Wader. "They blew me up, Crabba!"

"You blew yourself up," Crabba pointed out. "It was your mine on the Superchase Space Race finishing line."

"If you don't shut up," said Dark Wader, "I will barbecue *you* instead."

Another spacecraft flew level with Dark Wader's Squid-G. It was bright red and twinkled with jewels. At the helm was an angry-looking pig-shaped alien with heavy jewels in his butterfly-like ears.

Dark Wader pressed a button on the control panel. "What about you, Skyporker?" he growled through the intercom. "Have you seen those penguins yet? I'm going to blow them up like fish-flavored bubble gum."

"If I see those black-and-white bandits, I'll blow them up *myself*!" screamed Anadin Skyporker, revving his red spacecraft a little faster. Anadin Skyporker, emperor of the planet Sossij, hated the Space Penguins almost as much as Dark Wader did. "No one stops *me* from winning *my* Superchase Space Race and gets away with it!"

One of the control panel screens started blinking.

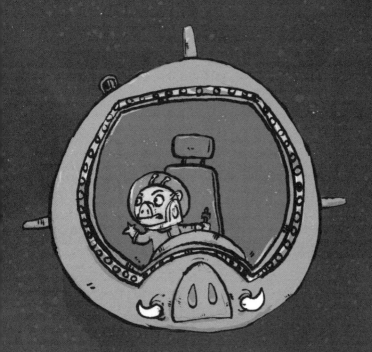

"Message coming through from our jellyfish-cam aboard the *Tunafish*," said Crabba, sitting up straight. "We must finally be in range."

"At last!" Dark Wader said eagerly. "What does it say?"

SPACE PENGUINS HEADING TOWARD PLANET KROESUS IN SECTION L OF THE UNIVERSE. CREW VULNERABLE TO ATTACK. REVENGE NOW OR NEVER.

Dark Wader thumped the control panel with delight. A couple of buttons fell off with a clunk. "We've got them, Crabba! Ask your jellyfish-cam why they're so vulnerable."

Crabba scuttled to the control panel and typed in the question.

WHY VULNERABLE?

There was a pause. An answer popped up: BURD FLOO.

Dark Wader laughed with glee. "That's

not something I have to worry about. Not now that I'm a pengbot. We have them like eggs in a frying pan!"

Crabba frowned. "I don't think that's how you spell 'bird flu,' boss."

"So what? Spelling never changed anything. Alert our entire Squid-G fighting force and set the coordinates for Section L immediately!"

"I'm summoning squadrons of X-jets from Sossij, too!" Anadin Skyporker screeched into the intercom. "We'll fillet them like flounders. We'll smoke them like kippers. Wait for me!"

CHAPTER NINE

FIGHT, FIGHT, FIGHT

"I hope I spelled 'bird flu' right," Splash said.

"Let us know the minute you see any Squid-Gs, ICEcube," said Captain Krill.

A huge meteor rocketed past the wing-pong room window. With a great bang, it burst into flames.

"This is the end," said Rocky.

"Disturbance in the space-time continuum, Captain," said ICEcube. Two more mechanical meteors exploded nearby.

BANG! BANG! "A fleet of Squid-G fighters and X-jets just leaped ten million light-years to join us."

"The message worked!" cheered Splash. "Dark Wader's on his way! The Dogmutts will have to turn back to fight him off. I'm a genius!"

"Wait — did you just say Squid-Gs *and* X-jets, ICEcube?" asked Captain Krill. "X-jets, as in the Emperor of Sossij's elite space-fighters?"

"Affirmative, Captain."

"How many?"

"Sixty-two," said ICEcube. "Plus thirty-eight Squid-Gs."

"I've found the flaw in our plan," said Captain Krill. "It's not just the Dogmutts aboard the *Tunafish*. It's *us*, too! And now that Skyporker's helping Dark Wader, we have a hundred spaceships all wanting to blow us up."

The Space Penguins stared at each other. It *was* a problem.

PYOW! PYOW!

PYOW! PYOW! PYOW!

"Beaky's space guns!" Rocky shouted.

"We need to take matters into our own flippers, crew," said Captain Krill. He peered out through the wing-pong room window. "We can't just sit here and wait for Wader and Skyporker to finish us off."

"Then let's go!" said Splash. He dashed to the door.

"We're locked in," Captain Krill gently reminded the ship's engineer.

"Duh," said Fuzz.

The ship's engineer waddled away from the door over to a small cabinet. He opened it and rummaged around before finally bringing out a silver key on a string marked: WING-PONG ROOM SPARE KEY.

"Is that what I think it is?" Rocky said in

amazement as Splash fitted
the key into the lock.

"I've kept the spare key in
here ever since the captain
beat Beaky at wing-pong
and Beaky locked him in for
revenge," Splash explained.

"You mean, we could have
gotten out of here ages ago?"
demanded Fuzz. "Why didn't
you say something?"

"It wasn't necessary,"
Splash said.
"Now it is."

The hatch
opened with a
gentle click.

The Space
Penguins
peered out.

"YOU DO NOT HAVE PERMISSION TO ENTER THE KROESAN ATMOSPHERE," boomed the intercom. "TURN BACK OR PREPARE TO DIE."

"What a nice welcome," said Fuzz. "Penguin power!"

He leaped at the Dogmutt Fuzz, flippers at the ready. *CLONK!*

"I almost feel bad about that," he added as the Dogmutt penguin keeled over and hit the floor beak-first. "He was a lot smaller than me."

"He's exactly the same as you, Fuzz," said Rocky. With a karate-chop, he knocked his double's flippers away from the control panel. "That's the point."

CHONK! CLUNK! THUNK!

"No way am I that small!" Fuzz yelled.
He leaped through the air feet-first and sent
the Dogmutt captain flying.

"Keep talking, crew!"
shouted Captain Krill. He
was fighting hard with
the Dogmutt Splash.
"These guys only
have about three
things to say!
That's how we'll
know who's fighting who!"

"What's the capital of
Norway?" asked Splash.

"This ship needs refueling," said
the Dogmutt captain.

"Wrong!" shouted
Splash. He stomped on
the Dogmutt captain's
webbed feet.

"I didn't know that one, Splash," said Captain Krill, his feet and flippers a blur. "Try something easier next time. Take *that*, you dog-faced dogfish!"

"Space-spinach is the worst stuff ever!" shouted Fuzz. He flew at the Dogmutt Splash, knocking him out with a single ninja chop.

"Check," said the Dogmutt Splash, just before he slid to the floor.

"Splash?" Fuzz prodded the unconscious penguin at his feet. "That's not you, is it?"

"I'm over here!" The real Splash was now engaged in flipper-to-flipper combat with the Dogmutt Rocky.

"Phew," said Fuzz. "That 'check' thing could have gone either way."

PYOW! PYOW! BANG-SPLAT!

Dogmutt Fuzz got back on his feet.

Captain Krill danced out of the Dogmutt's way. "What is that smell?" he asked.

"A slop-gun cannonball from a Sossij X-jet," Rocky said.

They were in the Kroesan meteor field now. Huge flaming rocks were hurtling past the windshield. X-jet slop guns shook the air. The smell of burning pig slop was terrible.

"Open the garbage disposal chute, Captain!" Fuzz shouted. He shoved the Dogmutt Fuzz hard in the belly. "Bye-bye, barnacle-brains!"

The Dogmutt's penguin shape dissolved, leaving nothing but a smoky dog-shaped figure that floated down the garbage chute.

"Right on target!" Splash shouted. He heaved the Dogmutt Splash up and pushed him between his feathered shoulders. "You're next, my goggled friend!"

CLONK! A second smoky-looking Dogmutt ricocheted off the chute walls and vanished. *BANG!*

"It's been a pleasure knowing me," said Captain Krill. He pushed the Dogmutt captain briskly into the garbage disposal chute.

Dogmutt Rocky swiftly followed. The Space Penguins just glimpsed his penguin feet turning back into smoky paws as the captain shut the door. *CLANG.* Then Rocky

turned a wheel on the wall. The airlock
opened, sending the Dogmutts into the
great black nothing.

"The *Tunafish* suddenly feels rather spacious," said Rocky, gazing at the cabin and the blinking flight instruments.

PYOW! PYOW! BANG-SPLAT! PYOW!

Flaming meteors whizzed past the window. The *Tunafish* shuddered and shook in the heart of the battle.

"Can we go now, Rocky?" said Captain Krill.

"I'll do my best, Captain!" Rocky said. He leaped into his pilot's chair. "Seatbelts on, everyone. Let's get the hecky-peck out of here to a spot of empty space where we can hit warp speed."

"Fly like you've never flown before, Rocky!" screamed Fuzz, hopping up and down in his seat.

"I'd prefer it if Rocky flew like he had flown before," said Splash. "Like, tons of times and really amazingly."

The Space Penguins gripped their seats as the *Tunafish* sprang upward like a trout leaping for a mayfly. A hundred Squid-G space guns and X-jet slop guns swiveled to follow the little spaceship.

BANG-SPLAT! PYOW!

Rocky made an impossible move, weaving through a wall of gunfire like a shadow. He then blasted a space cannonball into one of Skyporker's slop-gun cannonballs with an explosive squelch.

"Wahoo!" roared Fuzz.

Rocky slipped and whizzed and spun through the smoke. Nothing touched him. Nothing came close.

"Nearly there, Rocky," said Captain Krill. "One more burst of speed should do it."

"I'm the King of the Cosmos!" Rocky shouted with glee. The *Tunafish* jetted free from Kroesus's fiery meteors, the X-jets, and the Squid-Gs in a fish-shaped blur. "Warp speed . . . *away*!"

And *boom*. They were gone.

P.S.

"Where did they go?" demanded Dark Wader.

He peered out of the Squid-G windshield. The sky was full of burning meteors, but no fish-shaped spaceship could be seen. Squid-Gs and X-jets were flying around like mosquitoes with no one left to bite.

"The *Tunafish* was right there," squealed Anadin Skyporker into the intercom. "I was about to slop it out of the sky!"

"I think they warped out of here," said Crabba.

"Impossible!" shouted Dark Wader. "The jellyfish-cam said they were sick! You can't fly a spaceship like that when you're sick!"

Crabba clicked his claws nervously. "I told you 'bird flu' was spelled wrong, boss. The penguins must have found the jellyfish-cam and sent us a fake message. They tricked us. Again! I'm off to hide somewhere so you can't barbecue me." Crabba scuttled away.

"No!" Dark Wader yelled. "Skyporker, do something!"

"You do something!" Anadin Skyporker screamed back.

"How about I blow *you* up instead?" Dark Wader growled.

"Not if *I* blow *you* up first!"

The Sossij emperor swiveled his guns to point at Dark Wader. Dark Wader swiveled his guns to point at the Sossij emperor.

"I knew this was going to end badly," said Crabba, clambering back onto Dark Wader's shoulder to get a better look.

"Ready," barked Skyporker.

"Aim," snarled Dark Wader.

There was a pause.

"Hey, you there!" The Sossij emperor suddenly sounded shocked. "Weird smoky guy! What are you doing on my ship? Why is it so cold in here?"

"I was about to ask the same thing," said the pengbot, his laser eyes brightening with surprise. He stared at the dog-shaped visitor who had silently appeared in the Squid-G cabin.

"Oh, poo . . ."

"Destination: planet Kroesus," said the Dogmutt Dark Wader, settling into the controls. "Estimated duration of flight: eight minutes. Estimated time of arrival: twenty-five hundred hours, Kroesus time."

The intercom crackled.

"Check," the Dogmutt Anadin Skyporker replied.

TAKE A PEEK AT THE NEXT ADVENTURE:

SPACE PENGUINS
STAR ATTACK!

LOADING...

Welcome aboard the spaceship *Tunafish*. This is your Intergalactic Computer Engine speaking. You can call me ICEcube for short.

I'm here to guide the *Tunafish* through the universe, scan the galaxy for meteor storms, and spot any black holes. My penguin crew would have flapped their last flap years ago if it wasn't for me.

Penguin crew? Yep! Penguins are perfect for space missions. They're good at swimming (being in space is a lot like swimming), will work for fish, and are untroubled by temperatures near zero.

But why are these penguins in space? You'll have to ask NASA about that. Their finest scientists started a top-secret mission to send penguins farther and faster than any creature had gone before. They designed the spaceship *Tunafish* for all their needs. But the spaceship disappeared. Everyone thought that the mission had simply been a failure. Little did they know that the *Tunafish* and its penguin crew had just been sucked through a wormhole into Deep Space.

My database suggests that the best word for this is: whoops!

So now these penguins are traveling in search of a nice planet to call home. In the course of their quest, they've become intergalactic heroes. They've saved the cat race of Miaow from certain death on the planet Woofbark. They've even destroyed a large pair of frozen pants that was endangering space traffic on the tiny planet of Bum. They wouldn't have been so successful if it weren't for me, of course. Impressed?

There were five penguins to begin with, but the first mate, Beaky Wader, disappeared from the *Tunafish* three years ago after a nasty argument about who was going to be captain. The words "You haven't seen the last of me" echoed around the spaceship for days. Good riddance, I say. Beaky Wader was Trouble with a capital Fish.

And now — well, now they're still looking for the perfect penguin planet to call home. We'll probably be rescuing things as we go along, so I know you're as excited as I am to be here. Fasten your seatbelt and have a sardine. I would say that you are in safe hands, but penguins only have flippers.

Five. Four. Three. Two. One . . .

CHAPTER ONE

BOBBY CHEESE HAS A BAD DAY

"Help!" bawled Bobby Cheese.

The commander of the intergalactic pizza-delivery spaceship, the *Doughball*, was zooming toward certain death. A crazy-looking spacecraft had appeared out of nowhere, driving him off-course in a blaze of gunfire.

"Awaiting instruction," said the *Doughball's* computer.

"I am instructing you!" yelled Bobby Cheese. "Help me!"

He thumped all the buttons on the *Doughball's* shaking control panel in a panic. Bobby Cheese was a six-armed alien from the planet Bo-Ki, but even so, two thousand buttons took a long time to thump.

"Awaiting instruction," said the computer again. "Chill out, Cheese," it added.

"Don't tell me to chill out!" Bobby Cheese wailed. "We're hopelessly out of control!"

Stars shot past the *Doughball's* windows at weird angles. Bobby Cheese moaned. He didn't know if he was upside down or right side up.

"Awaiting instruction," said the computer for the third time.

"You're useless!" cried Bobby Cheese. "We have nearly a thousand pizzas flying around in the back. They'll be ruined. We'll be picking mozzarella out of the fuselage for weeks unless we get this ship back under control!"

"We'll be picking you out of the fuselage as well," the computer said helpfully.

"Quit the small talk and get me out of here," Bobby Cheese yelled. "Do you have any idea who's attacking us?"

The computer was quiet for a second. "The attack is by Squid-G fighters," it said at last.

"Squidgy what?"

"Squid-G fighters. Spacecrafts with considerable firepower and a strong fishy smell."

"But why are they attacking me?" shrieked Bobby Cheese.

"For fun?" suggested the computer.

The *Doughball* spun faster. Its nose dipped farther. The stars outside grew stranger. Bobby Cheese glanced at a tattered poster stuck on the wall. The poster showed four penguins posing beside a fish-shaped spacecraft.

"Only the heroic astronauts of the *Tunafish* can help me now," he said. "We have to contact them!"

"But they're just penguins," said the computer. "Are you sure you want to put your life into the flippers of four flightless fowl?"

"They're not just penguins!" cried Bobby Cheese. "They're space-fighting heroes! If I haven't died by the time they get here, remind me to get their autographs!"

The strange stars suddenly disappeared from view altogether as the spinning *Doughball* plunged into a bank of mist. Bobby Cheese typed a shaky distress call to the spaceship *Tunafish* and pressed send. Squinting desperately through the windshield, his eyes widened at the sight of a gigantic five-pointed star looming ahead of him.

"What's that? Is it a planet?"

"Planets don't have pointy parts. That's a space station," reported the computer.

The air filled with a humming sound. Bobby Cheese groaned and pressed his hands to as many of his ears as he could reach. It was all over. The *Doughball* was doomed.

Where was the *Tunafish* in his hour of greatest need?

ABOUT THE AUTHOR

LUCY COURTENAY has been writing children's fiction for a long time. She's written for book series like The Sleepover Club, Animal Ark, Dolphin Diaries, Beast Quest, Naughty Fairies, Dream Dogs, Animal Antics, Scarlet Silver, Wild, and Space Penguins. Additionally, her desk drawers are filled with half-finished stories waiting for the right moment to emerge and dance around. In her spare time, she sings with assorted choirs and forages for mushrooms (which her husband wisely refuses to eat).

ABOUT THE ILLUSTRATOR

JAMES DAVIES is a London-based illustrator, author, and pro-wrestling expert who grew up in the 1980s and loved to draw video-game bad guys and dig in the garden for dinosaur bones. Since then, James has gone to college, gotten a haircut or two, and is extremely busy working on all kinds of book projects.

GLOSSARY

ACCELERATE (ak-SEL-uh-rate)—to get faster

DESTINATION (des-tuh-NAY-shuhn)—the place a person is traveling to

DISSOLVE (di-ZOLV)—to disappear slowly, to fade away

DURATION (duh-RAY-shuhn)—the time during which something lasts

GAUGE (GAYJ)—an instrument that measures something

IMPOSTOR (im-PAH-stur)—a person who pretends to be someone else in order to trick others

INTERCOM (IN-tur-kahm)—a system of microphones and speakers that allows people to talk to others who are in a different place

PREEN (PREEN)—to clean or arrange feathers, done by birds with their beaks

SUSPECT (SUHS-pekt)—a person who is believed to have done something wrong

UNCONSCIOUS (uhn-KAHN-shuhss)—not awake and unable to see, hear, or think

VAST (VAST)—very large in size or amount

VULNERABLE (VUHL-nur-uh-buhl)—when a person or thing could be easily hurt or is unprotected

DISCUSSION QUESTIONS

1. The Space Penguins really dislike space-spinach. What kinds of food do you not like?

2. The Space Penguins talked to each other while fighting the Dogmutt imposters so they could know who was the real crew. Can you think of any other ways that the penguins could tell the difference?

3. What do you think will happen to Dark Wader and Anadin Skyporker? Will they be able to get back control of their ships?

WRITING PROMPTS

1. Would you like to become an astronaut? Write about why you would or would not want to travel in space.

2. The Dogmutts came very close to landing the *Tunafish* on Kroesus. Write a story about what would have happened if the space pirates had robbed the planet. What would the Space Penguins do?

3. Splash had his favorite type of cake, a supernova sardine cake, for his birthday. Describe your dream birthday party, and don't forget to describe the cake!